Jan Wahl

CATS AND ROBBERS

pictures by Dolores Avendaño

Tambourine Books New York

The text type is Esprit.
The illustrations were painted using
acrylics and colored pencils on paper.

Library of Congress Cataloging in
Publication Data. Wahl, Jan. Cats and
robbers / by Jan Wahl ; illustrated by
Dolores Avendaño.—1st ed.   p. cm.
Summary: When she lets lots of cats into
her house to get rid of the mice that are
keeping her awake, old Mrs. Mudge finds
that she has a new problem on her hands.
[1. Mice—Fiction. 2. Cats—Fiction. 3.
Robbers and outlaws—Fiction. 4. Stories
in rhyme.] I. Avendaño, Dolores, ill. II.
Title. PZ8.3.W133Cat 1995 [E]—dc20
94-48075 CIP AC ISBN 0-688-13042-9

10 9 8 7 6 5 4 3 2 1
First edition

Old Mrs. Mudge
sat up in bed.
"There are ghosts in the house!
Ghosts in the house!"
Mrs. Mudge said.

Shadows dancing,
footsteps prancing.
Creeping closer
around the bed.

There were squeakings and rustles,
eeking and bustles.
She pulled the covers
right over her head.

Mrs. Mudge peeked
and saw it was mice.
"Mice need traps.
Traps that snap.
Mice are not nice."

She put traps on the stair,
traps on a chair.
"I must catch them
at any price!"

The clever mice
quick as you please
skittered up walls,
scooted down halls,
and stole all the cheese.

Mrs. Mudge sighed.
Mrs. Mudge cried.
"Give me some peace!"
she prayed on her knees.

Yowling and meowling
right by the house
came a passel of cats.
"It takes a cat
to catch a mouse!

"I'll open the doors
and the windows, of course.
Come, kitties, come
into my house."

With a thump and a bump,
cats leaped inside.
Mrs. Mudge counted seven,
eight, nine, ten, eleven . . .
and ran to hide.

"Cats!" said the mice.
"Cats are not nice!"
They rushed to the door
and slipped outside.

Hither and yonder
cat feet prowled.
Tails to the sky,
whiskers high—
prowling cats yowled.

Down under the bed
Mrs. Mudge held her head.
"It gets worse and worse!"
poor Mrs. Mudge howled.

At last the cats paused
to lick their fur.
"We don't care.
We don't scare,"
they began to purr.

"Shh!" called the cats.
"There's something out there."
Then they all stopped
to sniff at the air.

Some robbers arrived.
One nudged a tall brother.
"The coast is clear!"
"Don't push, do you hear?
I'll tell our mother!"

In they dashed—
in they crashed—
one robber brother
after another.

This way and that,
in every nook—
robbers met paws.
Paws with claws.
The whole house shook!

Tripping, flopping . . .
flipping, bopping . . .
Down, and up!
Cat and crook.

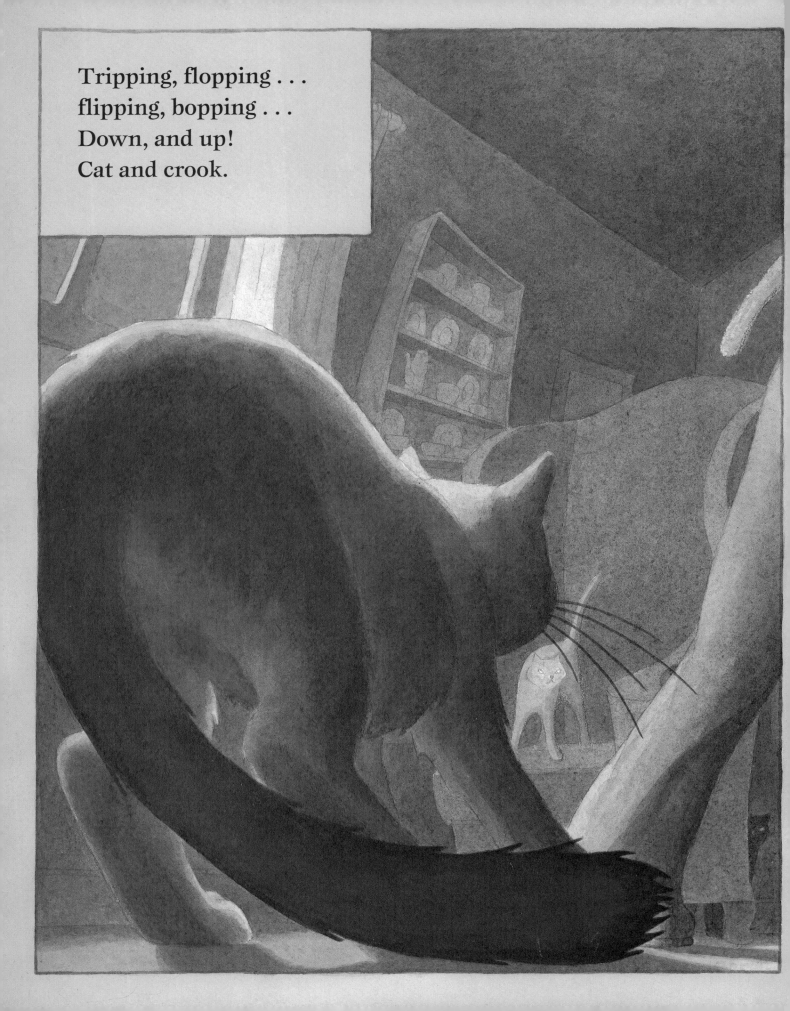

This was too much
for Mrs. Mudge.
She roared a roar:
"That's it! No more!
Nobody budge!"

Armed with a broom,
she sailed out of her room.
"HERE I COME!"
yelled Mrs. Mudge.

"I'll count to three!
ONE . . . TWO . . ." she said.
Spring and sprang,
cling and clang.
Cats and crooks fled.

She locked all the doors
and the windows, of course.
And brave Mrs. Mudge
went back to bed.

She listened hard.
"Ah. Not a peep!"
She closed her eyes.
To her surprise,
she couldn't sleep.

She couldn't sleep.
"It's not the same."
She said it twice.
"Just not the same . . .

"BRING ON THE MICE!"

And they came,
and they came,
and they came,
and they came.

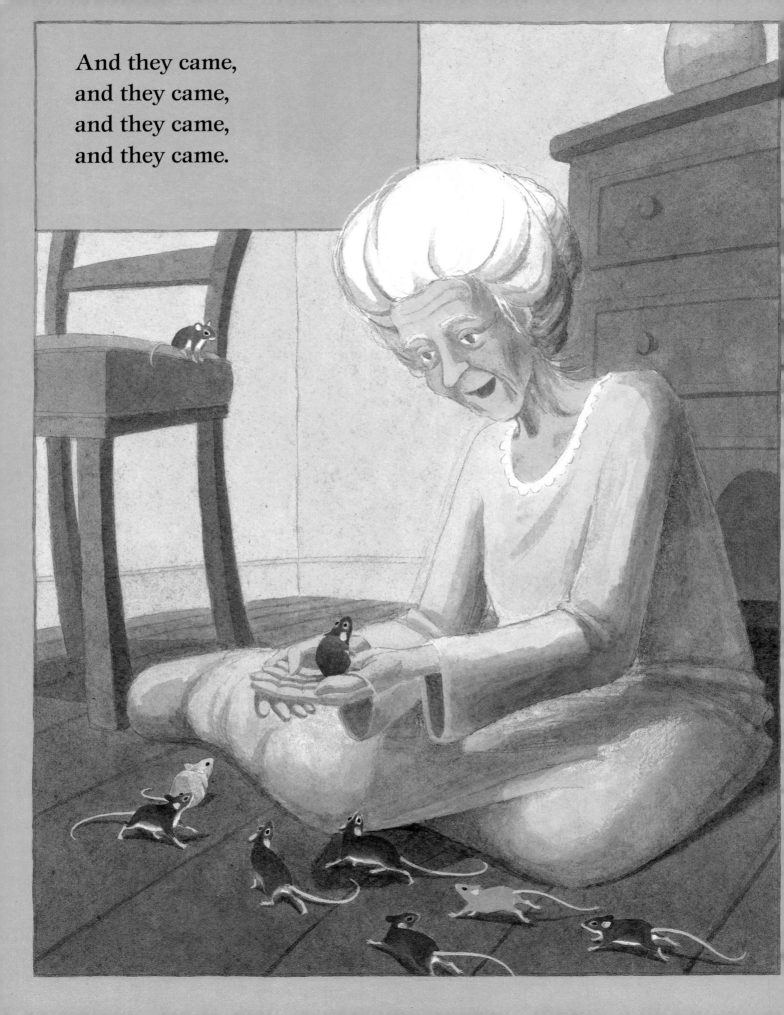

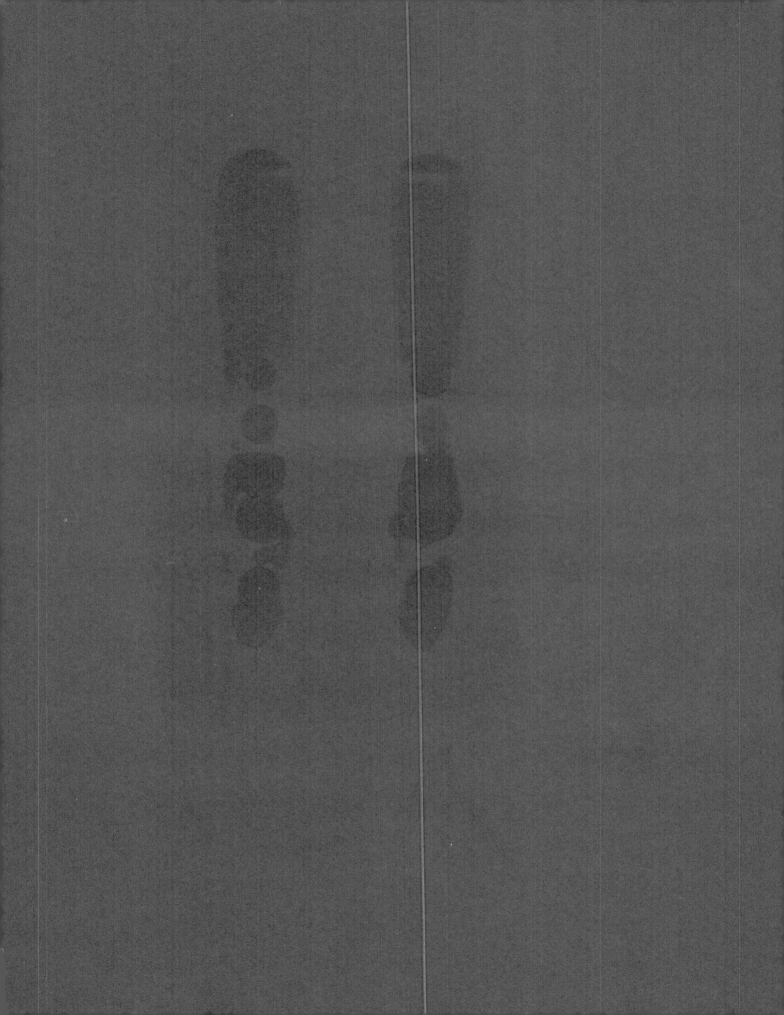